Horse Sacrifice
Charles Stein

Station Hill

Published by Station Hill Press, Barrytown N.Y. 12507,
with support from the Literature Program of the
New York State Council on the Arts & the National
Endowment for the Arts.

Produced at the Open Studio Print Shop in Rhinebeck,
N.Y., a non-profit facility for writers, artists &
independent literary publishers, supported in part by
grants from the New York State Council on the Arts &
the National Endowment for the Arts.

Photograms by Charles Stein.

ISBN 0-930794-30-3
      0-930794-31-1
First Edition
Manufactured in The United States of America

for Michelle

CONTENTS

 Horse Sacrifice

THE HUT

Through difficulties my spine
teaches itself rectitude
and a common line
from coccyx to cranium
inclining against the wind
permits
nothing not now the whole world
to fill its sail.

All my arguments
go up the beautiful alleys.

All the brackets break.   I sit
in the hut.
Only the wind
pushing the cloth
like a sail   out
from the window.
Only my song
that I permit
go on.

The gourds are in the box.

The little crystals   wrapped
in cloth
of many sizes
undisclosed.

Monads
I thought to answer
though none asked
indivisible into parts
yet multiple   each
on its purchase
including the whole.

Not yet put out.

The space of the hut itself a monad:
one window
opening
out.

The distinctive phenomena of the hut: how
increasingly this
shall
seem as a monad
is not
as yet
disclosed.

A sprig of maple bough
pushes in
the window
full of leaves.

I place the central stone upon the mat.

I sit on cushions in the hut
across
from the window.

The
"being" of
the items
never comes
apart
from
the items.

It is hidden
and yet
can   in
principle be
disclosed.

The items are hidden in boxes bags or shells
                                                            or
not yet having attained
an appropriate arrangement
lie out about other items
visibly busy though motionless
about the foot of the milk stool
near the stone.

Every item waits
its "being"
to arrive

but out of *what?*

Once in the new arrangement or
if ordered
in
an
ambiguous order

the "beings" flicker about among the items.

Odd window-curtain flickerings
emerge
from out of *what?*

All the old tunes
sing once more.

All the old dimensions
open about the stones.

The edges of the orders abrupt
before
an
indeterminate
source.

It is wide.   Illimitable.

We are looking
at the dark.

At night
to the west
there are pheasants
above the milkweed.

You are looking
at the dark.

Lightning bug phenomena.

When I pause   slow   poise
before the dark
of the valley

or when permit   frequent
minute
intervals
          edges of silence
about the sound
of words
in their concreteness . . .

I gather all my items into the hut
each in its old concreteness.

The new concreteness
of what it is
not yet determined
hence
its "being"
is not
disclosed.

I sit in the hut
doing some kind of
"contemplative excercise."
But this is false
solemnity. I sit
before
the stone.
But this is too solemn
a way
of introducing "the stone"
in the place of
the name for it.

Thunder rumbles off from what direction.

Midday airplane rumbling.
Coasting.
Wind.
Bird song.

Arriving.
Overwhelming.

From *what?*

Notion:

When "done"
that is
at
some
later time
after
many items have
been
variously shuffled about
or placed in a manner suggesting a certain arrangement
almost disclosed

if anyone should sit in the seat where in fact
I shall often have been sitting
while working out the placement
and arrangement
in the hut
            he
should become alligned
in a certain manner.

You must come into allignment
with the work
                otherwise
the "spirits" which rise
from the stone
are not of my doing.

In any case the sources
are dark.

The old Magistros
reel in the dark
winding airplanes in
across
the upper currents.

In Kelly's fantasy
the march of religious forms
and societies
moves across Asia
according to directives
or plots
of wise Magistros
east of the Caucasus
allowing the Christians to advance only thus far then
to recede
allowing the Buddhists further
wedging the Arabs
between.

In any case there would be a possible geometry
meting out the doctrines
according to the landforms
granting
variant
readings of "Being"
according to the destinies
of hordes.

All these *readings*
rise out of *what?*

They do not occur
apart from the landforms.
I borrow Ed Dorn's term for it.
The way Apache babies were initiate
according to Dorn
from birth
initiate
to the landform.

"Being"
is
in every case
the "being"
of
some item.

The "spirits" that rise from the stone
are none of my doing.

Yesterday Kelly remarked his own impatience
with the "intelligible"—the urge
to mumble and gesticulate
if only to hone out
the propitious tune.

The spirits rise out
as
that which is *known*
showing themselves.
                    A sylph
among wood sprigs
gold birds
wedges of copper and wrenches
rusted on the barn door
hooks
as heavy
as stone.

They are alive
as factors
of *our* lives
            flakes
from the entities
before whom
and for whom
they arrive.

They are not *merely* intelligible.

They flicker
as lives
out of the dark
fringed along silence.

Words begin to be strung like objects or items you
don't know what. You don't begin
at a center. You are moved
by peculiar
necessity.
Dogs arrive.
Or terrible horses break from their white corrals.
This is an omen.

I cannot designate or introduce at all
events from another history than this one.
History than this one.
If I could
clouds should interpose along about seven.
She works her parts.
I dream an exemplary
intercourse in Norway
with her.
I raid the rails.
There is an arbitrary thronging
of self-suggestive texts
each with its document
to be the next thing read.
Granted we read the world
what recommends the sequence?
Fate is ominous.
The bare back horses calm down as
the event for which their breaking loose was propitious is
resolved upon.
Thus it is read.
To read and to write are one.

"It only means that you shall conquer the world."

ARTEMIS

The simple facts
appear
in a stunning
manner.

Fresh
recurrent   there is
rebirth. Generations
die out   and
there are new
generations. H.D.
notices
flowers between
the railroad tracks
blossoming
during
the war
in London
in the constantly present demand. Wallace Stevens
notices
a star
that outlasts
war.

Now I am older   and
recurrent phenomena   appear
more
comprehensible   more
mysterious.

I mean something extra
drops away
and the facts themselves
reveal something
I had not thought so apparently
to be there.

Letting speech
relax
and deepen

the way the body
settles
in   gravity
takes over
the weight of the body
belongs to it   the air
runs through all our parts each
breath
interfuses
the world.

We are hung
suspended
and in that respect the interconnections
pre-exist their recognitions. This is not
visionary
in any *special* sense.

I don't want to attain
any longer   any
special
condition of the mind
and yet this is so because I see now
there is no
natural
stand point
in the sense of something common
something previous
some recognition
earlier than thought
common to all.

Primordial laughter.

Thick mist
out
the cabin
window
going through the trees.

      Some un-
familiar   animal call
out of the mist
               moving
close
to the hut.

We have already recognized
the startling   raucous
call of the tender
deer   so
that's not it.

Maybe raccoons.

Raccoons, possibly.

Language
of the goddesses.

The mind is so easily struck dumb. I become
thrown out of balance so easily
loosely
speaking
of the goddesses.

Golden quivers.

She is tall
and a shaft
of light.

Suddenly I become a member of an alien company.
Strange negotiations
procede in a language
similar to one I know
but slightly *off*. The content
is *almost*
foreign to me. I am naive again
and have to improvise
impromptu recognitions
dead-reckoning-like
just to go on listening.

She is like light
and larger than the whole forest altogether.

She produces
from the material of the forest—
earth, rock, wood, mist, seasonal
transformation—all
the small wood beasts.

But she also
in the hymns and old accountings
is said to stalk in the hunt with rampant joy
letting her arrows fly by day
among the panicking animals—
promiscuous slaughter.

One day the deer
stopped on the rocky
road outside the cabin
looking, we thought, for a salt-lick
or liking the taste
of the stones.

You were outside
and their eyes stopped you
previous
to bounding
away.

I am a small
raccoon, suddenly.

Watching
from under a tree
in the sudden angle of light
the visible

goddesses.

MINT

1

    Universals   Not
particulars.
            Particles.

Little clean white rocks in a small array
laid out along fragments
   from the inner sheen of clam shells.

The Head Man   is not a Man   and
he is not *like* a Man.

He does not have the problem about particulars. He is *only*
everyone *only*
the rigor
which sources
the entire
world.

We are exasperated to think him
                    standing
out upon his rock
(his rock which is not a rock)
exasperated   at the problem of ourselves.

We are standing
where the wave pulls back
   on shifty sands.

I am standing

on a *plank*.

23

They are not moods.

Perhaps these changes   more   are
motions in the substance of a glass.

Sludge. Stuff. Muck. Bits. Parts.

It is Not a new kind of water Not
something gaseous or *like* something
pervasive like gas is—

Not some new kind of rock or odd
possibility like stone Not
that it glitters Not that it remains
the same
in appearance
even when before it
all else
suffers change.

It is Not
           discriminated
                      out
of all else which *is*
                discriminated
                           out.

We engage
its circularity.

We introduce it
but then refuse it. It
remains. We
remain with it.

We are riding
out
on the mountain

3

He gapes
across the wood.

The measured
portion
of the dark
shapes
the rock pile.

The rocks are damp
and dark. A leaf
leans
at the window.
                    Scattered
parts
of clam shells showing
the shaded purple
inner parts
of clam shells rest
in a heap.

Small white stones spread out.

Dark
        release
        release
the dark.

Red stones shine on the shells.

Grey shells black shells white shells heap.

Reliefless   shadowing of things
in the hut. Not
plain. Not at all plain. Not at all
clear.   Not at all well founded. Not
disclosed.

The explanations are Not
explained.
      All the scholars
become so small
each now stands on a rock.

   There is an enormous
heap of tiny stones and
the ledges where each
of these exposed stones shows
to the partial window light
               one scholar

become that small
sits out
and cooks
one fish.

4

I become
the moonlit air.

The crescent of the new moon
hangs
in the west
between the end
of the forest and
the cliff
behind which
the sun just set.

I am not a local point out
in space there   I am the whole
air   I am blue   clear
and broad.

I journey through myself.

I gape across the wood.

                    And *things*
which are called by the names of things
slant along the penetration of my glance
into the open light
along the hill.

POP!

Deer hide out. A bug
with red cross-marks
climbs
a natural
stone.

I am spread thin a mist
smothering the sight
of the forest
                and things
recommend them-
selves
        as
swelling
black
hulls.

                    5

Wet, the roof leaks. Puddles
stain the wood grain. Odors
grow out from the rug.

In the camel-skin satchel
sopping so many days   white
mist-like fungus growths
spread over hidden stones.

Dank. Dark. Thick.

Mint leaves ring the cushion and repell
ants
to whom
        mint
is abhorent.

The ants no longer come close
when I sit
in the hut.

THE ARTISAN

I am sitting
in the office
on the hill
going up
from town.

And the light
is delightful
even though the trees are very thin
and it is a warm day
and this morning
when we were sitting out on the platform
in front of the house
the wind blew cold.

I was sitting in the hut and the sun
has moved so far to the south now the sunlight
comes into the hut
through the south window
at noon.

I am raunchy, anxious, upset. Thoughts
root up
jar and thrash

and I have only to wait
in the minute spaces between them
seeking release.

In the old days I'd've said
seek the sun.

I seek myself as if I seek the sun.

But I am no sun now.
I am there
like a wall
rising up and expanding in the dark

in back of
the scintillating nervous radiation
that animates the ground
in which thoughts sprout.

They sprout and sprout
from invisible root
contradictions

and the sun is too bright in here.

An elephant
is walking through the woods
thrashing the trees.

The leaves are loose and dry
and as he passes
he smashes the tree trunks
with his elephant trunk
and the dry leaves shake loose.

The soul cannot pry loose
and the elephant
becomes the whole sky.

I imagine an elephant
thrashing in the woods
with his trunk
and scattering the forest
beside him as he lunges and storms
through the woods
in the direction of the hunters.

I am like a wall.

I stop
and stop to examine but no I cannot stop
and I am like a wall

and the wall grows tall
and wide

and the energies are thrashing
in front
and the mind is bristling
to contain itself.

The elephant is standing
in the still sky
and regains the majestic posture
of his marching.

This hut is like a bottle
or like some box
and the intricate hands
of some Chinese artisan
manipulate the gems.

He has magical servants to work for him—
humanoid genii or gnomes
who enter the box
and place
            items
on the stones for him.

But this morning the artisan is disturbed
in his energies
and seeks to calm the winds
and he orders the movements of his elephants
to halt post haste
and the genii have to sit still
for long forced meditative stages.

I am an elephant
and I poise myself delicately
according to some intricate
training I've received
at the hands of Chinese artisans.

31

I poise myself and balance
on top of the box.

I become minute
and enter the hut
and balance
among the stones.

My body is like a bottle
and the light
suffuses the glass
but bends in its dents and chips
so particles of the light
thrash about
and I have to work to settle all the particles
at the bottom of the bottle
as though the light were substance
and I must summon my ten thousand artisans
to assemble the luminous parts
and drop them
with minute preciseness
each in its place
at the bottle bottom.

Then the particles of light begin to shine again
and the bottle becomes my body again.

I am only water now, only flow.

And the light is reductive to water
and the bottle
becomes some sac
and I am a bag of moist organic organizations
which operate according to some deep law
and there are circulations
throughout the space of my body

and I am some elephant
and the elephant is carrying bottles
to some Chinese locality.

The bottles are filled with homuncular artisans
trying to grow large enough each to escape the membrane
of the particle
in which he is compelled to radiate
according to some law.

Each artisan operates as the nucleus of some one particle
and his intelligence scintillates
fragments of the light. And the whole body shines
on the back of this majestic elephant.

The elephant is walking through the forest
and it is autumn
and the sun is hot
but the wind is blowing the leaves away
and the artisan
is cold.

And in order to preserve his bodily temperature
he performs some dazzling meditation feat
as he balances
at the head of his caravan
and each new tree that passes
is some new thought that rises
and offers the possibilities
of the things which droop from its branches.

I am an artisan
and I want to gather the gems
which hang from the trees.

I am a wall
and all the water that scintillates
in the great expanse in front of me
casts its tiny shadows
against me.

I rise
in back of myself
and listen
for the noises
in the wall.

The sky is like an elephant
and the wall
on which the cold wind casts
the shadows of hanging gems
and blows the thoughts of artisans
into so many particles
begins itself to loose
and yield its elements.

Stones and bottles speak

in the space of the hut.

BUS TRIP

1

Blank place.

Tiles and plastic seats
late at night
in a bus terminal

and a crazy drunk paranoid
who used to be standing outside on the bus platform
now comes into the terminal
and bothers people.

It is late at night
and the bus
which is going to go to New York from this bus terminal
has not yet arrived here.

The terminal room is a blank place.

The lights are bright in here
and fill every corner
and all the people who wait for buses
late at night
are not much bothered
by the bright plastic luminescence
of the bus terminal.

I need to do
something
so I walk
doing a walking
meditation excercise
for several moments.

I am walking up and back in a bus terminal.

I am only walking noticing
according to the meditation excercise
the movement
of my feet
across the floor.

I am not doing anything at all
except walking
back and forth across the plastic
floor of the bus terminal waiting room
and as I approach one wall
I stop
and turn slowly
and then I continue walking
across the floor of the terminal building.

It is late
and they are announcing now
the building is about to close.

2

The night is very simple and includes
everyone on the bus.
And something
as large as the night
is flashing
across
even this fellow sleeping
in the bus seat
to the left of me.

The driver turns out the lights
and the bus is going somewhere now.

The night is flashing
across the bus route.

And no one is doing anything.

3

In the restaurant
along the highway
some of the passengers get out to take
their rest stop.

The music goes on all night
and I strike myself
as crazy
because I try to attach the expression
of the music to something
trying to express something.

The motor on the bus keeps running
and the stop
is not a scheduled bus stop but
the whim of the driver
who needs coffee
or just wanted to get something to eat
so the sovereignty
of the driver
manifests
in the night.

Everyone accomodates himself
to the driver's
power.

4

At the next stop
he doesn't turn the lights on.

I am refreshed
and sit up alert
in the dark
and am clear now.

It is a late period
and the Empire
is yet
in power.

I have a certain freedom
regarding my overview.

I become a woman.

5

I become a woman
and I turn my ring
about the finger of my hand so the jewels
show only to my closed
palm. The dull gold
band shines outward.

I open my palm
but turn it face down
and I pass my opened
hand
across your body.

I remember doing this.

6

I sit
and keep going over
the same thought.

I am buried
at the bottom
of an animal
who cannot stop
breathing

38

and I accept this.

I do not attempt to force my beast, my captor
to stop this interminable
rising
and falling
of the breath.

I am at peace
and reconciled
and I come to rest here.

Everything is green
and light fills the spaces
between the most crowded
of possible circumstances.

That which goes before
and that which towers yet ahead
is
enormous. An endless voyage.

One has only to glance
in the direction of that which surrounds
to see that it is enormous *that* way

and there is no end to elements
and details
which gather outward
from the bottom of the breath
outward beyond the skin
and fill the air.

There are politics forever
and always another
town.

7

Much later in the night.

Four o'clock.
The empty empty
subway stop.

The porno stores flash off
except for two of them
and most of the movies
are shut down
but a whore
stops me
when I come out of the terminal
and on the subway steps
a man
with one of those hats
doesn't stop talking to a small
woman
and the sounds
don't stop
in the wires. Neons
buzz
without ever going off
and cars
up on the street
are audible
down in the subway.

Some woman
across the track
talks
and someone over on this side
walks all over the platform
clicking his shoes.

Dream at The End of a Bus Trip

A desolate part of an island.

A devastated land tract where vast
buildings are all torn down
and some of the people gather bricks
and old boards
from the ruin
and someone
with a round face
keeps making the bad decision
to go on drilling
in one distant corner of the place
proclaiming great lost money hoards
and in another
some husband
has died
and it passes as not to be remarked —
no one is to mourn the man —
even though a daughter asks the wife
wasn't there *some* good in him?
Wasn't his *body*
warm?

No one is to mourn the dead person.
The bodies are shut off from themselves.
And in order to maintain the Empire
the vast devastation must be preserved
and the drilling
must go on.

The man with the round face is crazy
and everybody hopes
the circumstance will not arise again in which
they have foreknowledge
he will command the drilling
to begin again.

He is outraged
and he owns
the devastated property.

And everyone knows
the digging into the dust of bricks and boards
must begin again.

I am walking
the enormous distance
of the island

and I seem to be the circumstance
that a man
with a round face
begins a drilling project.

He is crazy
according to what everybody imagines
and wishes to recover
his money.

The devastated area grows larger
though the space it occupies
according to the figure on the map
remains unchanged.

I am wandering further
to the west
of a devastated area.

The bricks are too small.
The boards are all too narrow.
A strange white heat
emanates irregularly
from certain of the building shells.

I am walking
through a devastated
area. All the buildings

are burnt out
and the boards
and bricks are coarse.

I am a devastated landscape
and my body
is coarse and raw.

The man with an oval forehead
is short and squat
and he persists
in conducting a drilling operation
into the rubble.

I am a squat stranger
with a round face
and I persist
in a drilling project
among the rubble of a devastated area.

I am searching among the rubble
and I come upon a round faced man
and later
I realize
that I am a round faced man
searching among the burnt out rubble of a devastated island
for hidden treasure. Someone has died
and there is gold
and other kinds of wealth
hidden among the rubble.

Later I realize
that I am the devastated
land operation. Irregularities
of heat
and light in the air
flash about my body. I am warm.
Parts of my body are warm
and parts flash
with a strange light. Parts

of me are brick and parts
are coarse burnt board.

I am searching in my body
as if among the parts
of a burnt out island.

There are hills to pass over and vast
tracts of land. Long buildings
made of coarse burnt wood
are black from the fire
but parts continue to glow red
and some parts give off
a strange white luminosity.

The air changes temperature
irregularly
because of the living
fire
in parts of the devastated buildings.

I am passing
through a devastated area.

Someone has died there
and a round faced man
the common people think is only crazy
digs in the rubble
for the money he has lost
so that the Empire
can go on.

I am passing
across a devastated territory.

I am gold
or wealth
or treasure
buried perhaps
in the still glowing rubble
of a devastated island.

The common people are scattered about in the ruins
of former structures
which still glow red and white
and a round faced man
is drilling
inspite of the pressure from the survivors that he desist
attempting to find me.

Some of the common people
are walking about in the rubble
trying to find me.
Someone has died.
And throughout the Empire
mourning is forbidden.

The details of a devastated landscape
stretch north and south
for many miles. The spaces
between the burnt out building shells
widen. There are gaps
in the silky black surfaces of the burnt
out building boards
and the devastated area
seems to grow wider
though the space included by its boundary
remains unchanged.

I am walking away
from a devastated
area.
It is night.

All the buildings are burnt out
but the wood and bricks of many of them
still stand.

I am making my way
to the west
back to the mainland
weeping profoundly

because of the child
of the dead man
mourning her losses
inspite of the ban. Irregularities
of temperature
coming out of the burnt out structures
forbid direct access.

I am walking westward.

Very few persons
occupy a devastated island.

One of them is crazy
and a man
has recently been cast off.

HORSE SACRIFICE

Alone
in a space made
entirely
of white gold

he breathed.

And the flakes
became parts.

And there was nothing
but these gold particles
departing from him.

And everything anywhere
was only himself all shining
without limit but
dense
and solid
gold.

This was the old gold light there was
when old gold light shot out
when an old man shoots gold light.

He was alone
within himself
and very old.

And everything was quiet there within him
and all there was
is
enclosed there
in this old
gold
but living
breathing
silent
knowing
being.

It spread out everywhere
and nothing happening in any part of it
wasn't part of it.

All of it
held together
and the movement
of the flakes
outward as it breathed
was an ordered
breathing
flow.

He was alone
and very old
and everything there was
is
his parts.

2

All the crows are up in the empty elm boughs.

Black birds pass
flapping
in the solid
gold
air.

The Old Gold Man is afraid
because of the sound
of his parts.

He moves
and the fringes
of the dome
rattle from below
and crows
and gulls
rush to fill up the spaces
in the waves he makes
and the sound of the birds are accommodated
as if they were sounds of his own.

3

He has the head of a dog or the head of a horse
and all his limbs and bodily parts
are all the other animals
and in his terrific panic he scrubs
himself with rough organic
stones scraping
the animals off from his body
until his fear is dissipated and beasts
are spread
abroad
everywhere
in an open arena.

He has the head of a horse
and the man
who was his first cast off
son
returns
with an ax
and cuts off the head
of a shining stallion.

It is the Vedic
horse sacrifice.

And the animal
wild arena
becomes changed
because of the horse sacrifice.

4

What is it like in the hut?

Someone has entered and eaten the green away
from the cloth
and shreds hang down now
under rocks and statues.

5

When The Old Gold Man awoke in his gold abode
even though alone he was afraid.

There was nothing else possible anywhere.

Nothing was outside the globe he was.

His reasoning
was waves
or filaments
in golden substance.

The birds he saw
began with the movement
of his thought.

He shook himself

and a woman
ran
away.

6

Now the earth is green and brown and shining

and I have a friend who thinks that stones
and mud and water
have
fearful
properties.

He says that there is lightning
force
in the body of ravenous animals and
that
this
same energy
springs in the limbs
of victims as they panic at merely the hint of attack
and flash
across
the forest.

Deer
run along the road
or stop
stunned
in the car-beam.

7

Is the Horse
the god?

The black head of the horse and the shining
eye
of the black head of the horse

or the plaster
mold of the stallion's head
with its curious
glinting
eye
in the dream I had
or in Cocteau's movie
I saw
the day after
the dream I had.

8

They cut off the head of the gangster's
favorite black stallion.

9

When they slay the horse with the broad ax
it is an act to diminish the power the gods have
and
to transmute
themselves.

10

The gangster leader keeps trained wild horses
and the wildest horse there is
stomps and bucks
about the corral
kicking and flailing his fine black mane
when any of the attenders attempts to soothe him
only the gangster leader
can stand
several paces away
and the horse
stops
struggling against his own extreme force
exasperated
at the logic of power
the gangster leader has
to stop him so.

11

My friend is not the person I thought he was.

He is probably an animal nature
who does not even come close enough for me to see or hear
but I *recall*
the information
he is.

His use
is to put at a distance
that which is too near.

He has a blue coat
and walks
in the strong wind
along a snowy path
lightly   not depressing the surface
of the snowfall but gliding
in a blue light
listening
for the distances
between his own
silent words
which are also

in a blue light.

12

The sacrifice cuts up the beast
and all the parts
and all the dissipated
energies
go
out into shapes specified
by the initial
ritual formulation.

The head of the horse is the sky the hoofs are the earth itself
the belly of the horse is the wind but the voice
that rises from the sac of his organs is only
the voices all animals have
and the man
in his blue coat
in the middle of winter hums
his intermittent hymns
and connects
because of the retroflection he can afford himself

to an opening previous to all initial scatterings
previous to the eye of the horse
which is the sun now low and gone
to the bones of the horse which are stars
the year is the body of the sacrificial animal
to the dawn
to the moon
to the genitals
to the ribs
to his floating
eye.

He walks
in a blue coat
and it is only some minor
dailiness
he performs.

He has to lift twigs here.
He has to cut reeds.
He moves this item
from out of this closed place
gives it air or dries it somewhat
according to the instructions of his consort or *she*
helps *him* lift *it*
in the early morning orange colored light
that comes over the snow.

13

There was nothing whatsoever in the beginning.

Everything had been taken absolutely away
back   through the original small doors.

And the paradigms had shimmered in the glassy heat.

All the ultimate conditions had been surpassed.

All the stones are placed in the places placed out for them.

All the paradigms have gone away.

And all the doors had gone away.

Everything had proceeded as far as anything can proceed,
                    come back again, and vanished again.

There was nothing whatsoever in the beginning.

There was a jewel
of only empty
spaces. All the distances
were themselves
and no measures
separated off
parts
of anything.   It was not
all bright
and all gold.

It was not even alone.

Someone was sleeping under a tree
and the temperature outside was the same
as the heat within.

Suddenly a goat
ran
up between long tree rows.

This was the first thing
there was.

MORE ELEPHANTS

The elephant
is walking
through the woods.

The rider
in his seat up there
marks every step
and every gluide.

The passages
between the trees
are slim
and the trees
arise before the gaze
of the elephant rider

but he keeps on riding.

Winter coming on.
                    Sun
bright
shines through south-east window
of the quaint hotel.

I rent a room up there.

I am sitting
on the carpet
and my body is like some mountain.

And the flashes and spasms
burn along the lacoliths
and basoliths
and new
passages
open
showing
mine veins.

I am mining passages in my mountain.

Bowels are gems
or store gems
and accurate systems of agony organize
according to the pressure
suffered by the stones.

I am sitting on the carpet
on the floor
in the old
hotel.

And every thought that rises
has
an elephant
moving
through the brush
underneath it.

He is moving his heavy legs a pace at a time
and the trunk
sways
according to the foreward motion.

I am a carpet of fens and bush
and the sunlight flickers
through the woods
striking the spaces
between me.

And every thought that rises
vanishes
according to the pace of the elephant.

I am mining
in my body
and uncover some endless disease.

I am in the wrong place.

All the organs
are squeezed by insidious design
and emit poisonous secretions
into themselves
which take long ages
to accumulate
effects.

I cause   penetrating radiations
to loosen the grip
of the mountain stones
upon the more valuable strata.

I am like the moon
and medicine the valley groves
with a cold white fan of light
tuning the inhabitants
to my lunar rock design
inspite of the fears they have.

An elephant is passing
through the valley groves.

And all of the people come out of their quaint hotels
in gross provincial admiration
to celebrate the majesty
and beg for money.

The people in a valley town
come out to admire the Emperor.

Fools and clowns are jigging
on the backs of elephants.

Every organ is like some hut
and the people are like secretions
that rush out to proffer demands.

And every Fool is like some thought
jigging on the back of an elephant.

The elephant is slow as a mountain
and his paces seem invisible
to the people who watch
for the shifting of strata
but the mountain takes long ages
to advance one step.

The fools have all grown silent
and move in accord
with the pace of the mountain.

And the moon comes out of a crack.

RK'S ELEPHANTS

They are walking
in the snow.

And the phrases
rise up
in desultory
fashion

and the phrases
are phases

and the fashions
are desultory
patterns
confounding
the phases

and all the phases appear
in each phase and every phase
is a pattern
of its phases

and I am a boat
out

and the sea
is a machine

and I can hear the whirring of wheels intimate
between the sounds of all my phrases
and there are minute lights
sparkling
dimensional
to speech

and the ocean is an elephant.

And all the speech that rises

flashes

from the thought
the ocean drives.

BEHIND THE HUT

He is waiting
in back of the shed.

He lifts a cup to his lips
but the water freezes instantly.

The sun looks odd.

She is standing upright in a small hut and
the sun breaks the old glass window so violently it is
just what it is
beyond this zone
a vicious blast
one false move
and agility becomes
futile gesticulation

the sun is a brittle object
ending the moment of its rising

the train goes by its riders

we vanish away
and the relations of entities scare us, dear

we hold each other up
and you are a damn fool
and I am a petulant bitch
and anyone at all is a nimble point of light
at the end of a beam
landing
among the tall grey stalks
or strange corn-stalk ghosts
stiff and dumbly triumphing
next to the tractor
in a land of snow.

We seek necessity
and so define a text
which provides a road
through many gates
and after each phase-like
step along the cobbles
the cobbles become the sea
and still the sun reflects
down on each particular.

You are not journeying alone now bodily stripped,
but, vehicular, you are a chariot
or pinto-wagon of yourself
and the time you take to go through each gate
might
seem
but
one millisecond longer
and memory
might over come you from behind changing
the roadway once more
to a sequence of animal dangers
and in order to prevent this
suddenly you are a boat
out
on a glorious sunlit ocean
channeled by supreme concentration of surging life
backwards
through

what
appears to be the only gate there is.

The text
is all at once

but the reader
is a seed
in a boat

or a gem
in an egg

or a cod
in a school

or a white bone
in a dark shoal.

He is covered by the vast shell
of the single item in his momentary idiolect.

He is the juicy pulp
within the problematical
tonus of the rind.

My cock is hard
and you touch it
at just the right spot
but I am withholding my seed
to elaborate our desire
and my mind
is the hand
I relax behind my back
and bring it into play
when I hear you humping
beneath the absence of my thought
and the embrace of a larger sentence
closes with you.

This is the house
from which the carpet
has been carefully taken back
and the servants are actually princes
and tzarinas
of the old regime
received and almost revivified
but nonetheless devout and loyal
and
whatever promised april street of youth
the noble beings decline
and seek about the proper beds and crannies
wherein they hunger
to fall to.

It is very still in here
and everything that moves
is
subject to a further investigation that reveals
the crystal light
spark
is gone
before it has a chance
to change into anything.

The snow is as slow as it is
and the small black bark slabs
are like what is left of myself
and take their place
among the ancient beds
along the snow.

THE END OF THE ELEPHANTS

I am to remember
not only the thought
but the elephant
that
it rides on.

My body is an elephant
because of how heavy it feels
to be brought down low
slow
into itself
the envelope
fits exactly
and I am to bring back the good coin
and restore to circulation certain minted capital
I am riding therefore in one of those bumpy cabanas
that fit on the tops of elephants
as they wander
with messages
I have not yet
coordinated quite
with prospective destinations
but nonetheless continue and must not delay
sorting out things and remaining
in whatever kind of motion
I find is going on
and I don't complain about the terrain
or other contingencies.

My body is an elephant and I fit into it
without any difference
at all.

SONG

in
   the direction
of
what
already guides the flow
through the matter
in which it
glows
      the sparks
of the deity
glint
on the broken pieces of blue
bottle glass neglected
in
the snow

the slow perfection increases
with the heat that grows in bags
expanding and contracting
in a regular watch

the hawks
come back
to the tops of the trees

black rivers run again under the slabs
of ice
    which
remain
connecting fallen branches

a different time a different rule?

variable regulae
grow in the matter the matter
is not black any more
in back of the watchful fortress
the bellows
reddens

the coals
the warmth
spreads

the hawks
are divided
by themselves
the mountain
has no parts
the containments open and the sky
colors open in the belly
of the furnace there is an azure
expanse
in the black rock wide

and *not* only sizzling blind white ghastly dangerous but
at the bottom
the goddess
is sweet blue
and her cells are the orders of the memory
by which the primes direct
construction
of the only adytum

in back

in the direction
of that from which
she flows

the girl
on the meadow
with her male
companions
who follow
and tease each other with the flower she is
within the impossible posture
her mouth is open
and her hand is rubbing a muscle
in the back of one of these while the other
is doing something delicate and precise
to the space below

71

THE LANGUAGE ...

creates itself.
The world
creates itself.
There are three women
molding clay.
Some of them are spinning
or weaving
or others do
other creative
tasks
with all the materials
there are.
The materials
create themselves
out of minutest
molecular
possibilities.
The molecules
create themselves.
All the possible forms
invisible within the primal
golden
ray
create themselves
within a space
encompassing everything.
There is an old gold man
encompassing all the creative possibilities.
All the destructions
of form and substance
interpenetrate themselves.
I am sitting in the house
and think to become as quiet
as anything there is.

I think to let
all the molecular displacements
continue and the one
fructifying
ray
penetrate
each consequent
condition
and I propose to follow the flow
thought upon thought
penetrating and residing
within each consequent
propositional state.
All the looms
are running at once.
All the clay wheels
are spinning
because of the action
of the foot of each
of the women
kicking the kick wheels
everything
is
at the same time
running by the continuation
of their own original energies.
All the destructions
continue at once.
All the thoughts
continue at once
and the language
includes the spaces
between the propositional acts.
I take up my place
and I let that same place pass
into the molten golden
sources of all possible propositions
and all the positions
continue
into their subsequent conditions.

All the gods
are singing at one time
and the music
is nonetheless
the consequence
of a single ray.

So then all the False Ones

are sitting on their chairs

which are like thrones

composed of enormous stone carvings

and because they look very much like indomitable
objects which can never
be moved by any force
the falseness itself
is swallowed
by that very indomitableness
and the conscious penetration
is not required
but the motionless gods
determine one possible set
of all the qualities there are
upon their stones.

A bird

in the shape of a person

a person with tunes

in his head

becomes the shape

of a molten

golden

ray

and the language of the women on the thrones

invokes their golden hearts

imploring these birds to descend now

and activate emotional natures

and to melt

the stones.

The stones are already

molten golden sources of themselves.

It is impossible.

It *is* possible because the jungle-like cartoon
goes on within the continuity
even of the stones.
The stones are enormous
and the indomitable
quality of the stones
includes
everything there is.
Everything there was
is included
by these stones
nonetheless their insides
are molten
golden
forces
and the ultimate constitution of all of them

remains
and impeccable
simplicity
and there is a jungle-like density of nervous
life
churning within its greenness and terrified
because of the night
noises and the sound
of animal musics invoked.
Everyone is warding off something
even in the subtlest centers of
civilized jungle life
the banishing rituals continue
into the morning light. Some magus
holds his dagger
with rigid out reach of his arm
and he carves the shapes
in the multiple direction of his will
intending to hold at bay
the radiant noises
which bellow from the east
in the shape of rhinocerous dangers
which bellow from the west
in the figure of some deep abyss
in the north
there is the sources all white abstract
and below
to the south
the jungle itself
is warming all life
with golden molten
manifestations seductive and sweet.

The language is creating itself to the south
and the sweetness pours over into the roots
and fruits
and the promise of dangerous conclusions.

This new proposition causes the magi to drop their daggers
and the women get up from their jug making
and fuck in the house with the scribes.

The womanly languages are making their pleasures
and they are lighting enormous furnaces
big as the sky.

Special thanks to Kris Hultgren, Patricia Nedds, and Frauke Regan for pre-press work; to Guy Fabia for press-work; and to George Quasha and Open Studio.